GOLDILOCKS
AND
THE THREE BEARS

RETOLD AND ILLUSTRATED BY
LORINDA BRYAN CAULEY

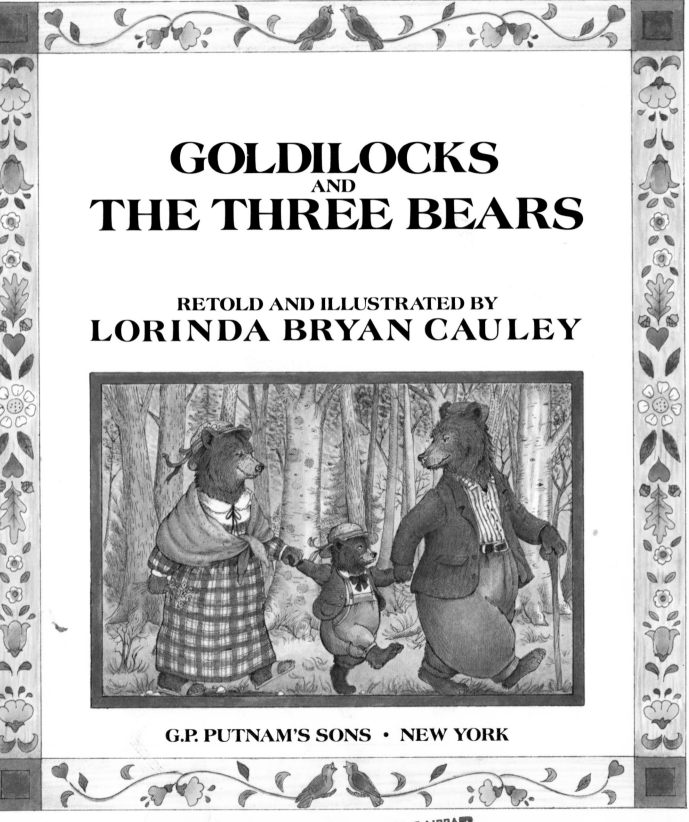

G.P. PUTNAM'S SONS · NEW YORK

Text and illustrations copyright © 1981 by Lorinda Bryan Cauley.
All rights reserved. Published simultaneously in Canada by
Academic Press Canada Limited, Toronto.
Printed in the United States of America.
First impression.
Library of Congress Cataloging in Publication Data
Cauley, Lorinda Bryan.
Goldilocks and the three bears.
Summary: A little girl finds the empty home
of the three bears where she helps herself
to food and goes to sleep.
[1. Folklore.   2. Bears—Fiction] I. Three bears.   II. Title.
PZ8.1.C25Th   823'.7 [E]   80-26253
ISBN 0-399-20794-5
ISBN 0-399-20795-3 (pbk.)
First Peppercorn paperback edition published in 1981.

for my son,

Ryan Patrick
born
Nov. 8, 1980

♥ with love ♥

Once upon a time in a cozy house in the middle of the woods, there lived three bears. One was a great big father bear with a thick shaggy coat, large paws, and a deep gruff voice.

The next was a mother bear with a soft fur coat, a middle-sized body, and a gentle low voice. The third was a little baby bear, with tiny furry paws, and a funny small voice someplace between a whine and a squeak.

One day after the bears had made their morning porridge and poured it into their bowls, they decided to take a walk in the woods while the porridge was cooling. They didn't want to burn their mouths by eating it too soon.

Now there lived near the edge of the woods, a little girl named Goldilocks. She was called Goldilocks because her hair was light and shiny gold. That morning her mother sent her out to pick flowers to keep her out of mischief. (Goldilocks was *always* getting into trouble.)

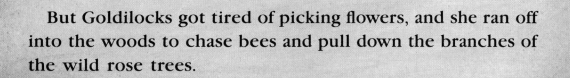

But Goldilocks got tired of picking flowers, and she ran off into the woods to chase bees and pull down the branches of the wild rose trees.

Before long, Goldilocks found herself in a clearing. Ahead of her she saw a pretty little house. Finding the door open, she peeped in, and, seeing nobody, she made up her mind to go boldly in and look around.

A delicious cinnamon smell was coming from the kitchen. On the table Goldilocks found three bowls full of oat porridge. Goldilocks was always as hungry as she was full of mischief, so she decided to taste the porridge. First she took a spoonful from the great big bowl, but it was too hot and it burned her mouth.

Next she took a spoonful from the middle-sized bowl, but it was too cold.

Then she took a spoonful from the wee little bowl, and it was just right. She took one bite, then another and another, and soon she had eaten up every bit!

Goldilocks looked around for a comfortable chair to rest in. She was feeling tired from all her running through the woods, and she was full of the delicious porridge. First she sat in the great big oak chair, but it was much too hard.

Next she sat in the middle-sized chair with the velvet cushion, but it was too soft.

And then she tried the little wicker chair and it was just right! She rocked and she rocked and she rocked until the bottom fell out, and down she came, *bang*, on the floor!

Now Goldilocks spied a flight of stairs, and she began to wonder what was upstairs. So up she climbed until she found herself in a pretty bedroom with three beds, side by side. Seeing the beds made her feel sleepy, so she decided to lie down and take a short nap. First she climbed up into the great big bed, but it was too hard and the pillow was much too big.

Next she lay down in the middle-sized bed, but it was too soft. She sank down so deep into the quilts that she had a hard time getting out again.

Then she tried the wee little bed, and it was just right! She snuggled down under the cozy quilt and fell fast asleep.

By this time, the three bears were tired and hungry. They were sure their porridge would be ready to eat, so they went home for breakfast.

When Papa Bear saw the spoon left in his bowl, he roared out in his great gruff voice, "SOMEBODY'S BEEN EATING MY PORRIDGE!"

Then Mama Bear looked over at her bowl, and she saw that it had been moved, so she threw up her paws and cried out, "Somebody's been eating my porridge!"

Baby Bear ran over to his porridge and saw the empty bowl. He squeaked, *"Somebody's been eating my porridge and has eaten it all up!"*

Now the three bears were sure that someone had been in their house, and they began to look all around the room. Before long, Papa Bear noticed that his chair was not as he had left it and he growled, "SOMEBODY'S BEEN SITTING IN MY CHAIR!"

Mama Bear went to her chair and saw a hollow in the middle of the cushion where Goldilocks had sat. She scowled and said, "Somebody's been sitting in my chair!"

Baby Bear ran over to his chair and saw that it was broken. He wailed in his squeaky little voice, *"Somebody's been sitting in my chair and has sat the bottom right out of it!"*

Papa Bear was in a rage, wondering who would dare come into their house without being invited. So huffing and grunting, up the stairs they all went to see if anyone was there.

When Papa Bear came to his bed and found the pillow pulled from its place, he roared out in a fury, "SOMEBODY HAS BEEN SLEEPING IN MY BED!"

Mama Bear looked at her bed and saw that it was full of lumps and rumples. She cried out, "Somebody has been sleeping in my bed!"

But when Baby Bear came to his wee little bed, the quilt was in place, the pillow was there, but on the pillow was Goldilocks' fair head, and she was fast asleep! *"Somebody has been sleeping in my bed,"* squealed Baby Bear, *"and here she is!"*

Baby Bear's sharp, shrill voice woke up Goldilocks, and she found herself nose to nose with the angry little bear. She sat up quickly, and when she saw the other two bears, she tumbled herself out the other side and flew across the room.

She took one look at the open window and jumped out, landing in the soft grass below. Goldilocks looked up to make sure she had not just been imagining things, and there were the three bears staring down at her. She got up and ran, but it seemed as if the woods were full of wild bears, so she ran faster and faster. She didn't look back once until she was well out of the woods and could see her own little house.

When Goldilocks was safe at home, her mother gave her a scolding she did not soon forget. And she made up her mind never again to make herself quite so much at home as she did in the house of the three bears.